Turbo and Chet are brothers, but they are as different as be. Chet loves his job as safety manager at the Tomato Plant. Turbo lives for speed. He wants to race!

Chet wants his brother to accept the truth. Snails aren't fast. "I wish you'd put all this racing nonsense behind you," Chet tells Turbo.

One evening, Turbo inches his way to the highway to watch the cars, trucks, and motorcycles zoom past. A gust of wind picks Turbo up and drops him on top of a car racing down a dry riverbed. At first he's a little afraid, but as the wind whips past him, Turbo starts to have fun.

"Faster!" he yells to the driver.

adapted by Maggie Testa

Simon Spotlight
New York   London   Toronto   Sydney   New Delhi

SIMON SPOTLIGHT
An imprint of Simon & Schuster Children's Publishing Division
1230 Avenue of the Americas, New York, New York 10020
DreamWorks Turbo © 2013 DreamWorks Animation, L.L.C. All rights reserved,
including the right of reproduction in whole or in part in any form.
SIMON SPOTLIGHT and colophon are registered trademarks of Simon & Schuster, Inc.
For information about special discounts for bulk purchases, please contact Simon & Schuster Special Sales at
1-866-506-1949 or business@simonandschuster.com.
Manufactured in the United States 0513 LAK
First Edition
1 2 3 4 5 6 7 8 9 10
ISBN 978-1-4424-8471-9
ISBN 978-1-4424-8472-6 (eBook)

The driver slams on the gas pedal and Turbo goes flying into the car's engine! All of a sudden a blast of nitrous oxide hits him. It winds its way through his body before Turbo roars out through the car's tailpipe.

The next morning Turbo wakes up dazed and confused, and he crawls home.

"I'm okay," he assures himself. But then two beams of light shoot out of his eyes, just like the headlights of a car!

Completely surprised, Turbo backs away and bumps into a table leg. His shell lights up and blares like a car alarm. *Woo-woo-woo!*

"What's happening to me?" Turbo cries.

Pretending everything is normal, Turbo heads off to work.

In the middle of Chet's safety meeting, his antennae pick up a radio station! Turbo slinks away, only to come face-to-face with a boy on a tricycle.

Just as the boy's tricycle is about to squash him, Turbo discovers another new ability . . . the best one of all. He has the power of superspeed! Before he's crushed, Turbo zooms away . . . fast!

The boy charges forward, startling Turbo into zooming up the trike's front wheel. In a panic, Turbo revs his engine. The wheel spins out of control, causing it to crash right into the Tomato Plant.

No snails are hurt, but the foreman at the plant is so upset that he fires Turbo and Chet!

Suddenly, a crow snatches
Chet and flies away. "Help! The
world is moving," Chet yells.
Turbo knows what he has to do:
Follow that crow!

Far across town, the crow drops Chet on the roof of an old taco truck. He is about to gobble Chet up when Turbo speeds in and knocks Chet out of the way.

"Am I dead? Is this . . . Heaven?" Chet asks as a plastic cup slams down, capturing the two snails inside.

"Buenas noches, little amigos," says the man holding the cup. His name is Tito.

Tito takes Turbo and Chet to Starlight Plaza. There are other shop owners there, and a small racetrack. Snails wearing fancy racing shells wait at the starting line.

"Little far from home aren't ya, garden snail?" a big snail says to Turbo. His name is Whiplash.

Then the flag is waved and the race is on! To Turbo's surprise, these racing snails aren't any faster than the garden snails back home.

Turbo revs his engine and *vroom!* He's off. A streak of blue light blazes down the track as Turbo zooms past the finish line.

Tito, the other shop owners, and the racing snails can't believe their eyes!

"What did you say your name was again?" one of the snails asks.

"My name is Turbo," he declares proudly.

Chet wants to go home and get Turbo fixed.

"I don't need to be fixed," Turbo explains. "There's nothing wrong with me."

"But you're a freak of nature," replies Chet.

"I know!" says Turbo. "Isn't it great?"

Tito is convinced that Turbo is a shooting star. The world needs to know about him. Turbo knows just how to make that happen. He wants to race in the Indy 500! Soon, the taco truck is on its way to Indianapolis!

The shop owners and the racing snails are excited. Only Chet is worried. "What happens if you wake up tomorrow and your powers are gone?" he asks Turbo.

"Then I'd better make the most of today, " Turbo replies.

INDIANAPOLIS

When the taco truck arrives at the Indianapolis Motor Speedway, Turbo is awestruck. There are racing cars and drivers as far as the eye can see. Tito goes to register Turbo in the race, but it's not as easy as he had hoped.

So Turbo takes matters into his own hands. He zooms around the track to show the world just what he can do!

FIRST LAP: 225 MPH
SECOND LAP: 228 MPH
THIRD LAP: 224 MPH
FOURTH LAP: 227 MPH

FOUR LAP
AVERAGE: 226 MPH

His four lap average is 226 miles per hour. The crowd goes wild!
"That's fast enough to qualify!" remarks Whiplash.
Turbo will race in the Indy 500!

"I'm begging you," pleads Chet. "Just quit while you're ahead."

Turbo shakes his head. "I've wanted this my whole life. All these people believe in me. Why won't you?"

The next morning, while everyone else heads off to the track, Chet stays behind. As he watches the taco truck pull away with his brother inside, a little boy scoops him up.

"You're going to have the best view in the house, little snail," the boy says as he carries Chet to a seat in the stands. Chet will have to watch Turbo's race whether he wants to or not!

Turbo's big moment has finally arrived. But the race doesn't get off to a great start for him. The huge cars cut him off and blast him with exhaust fumes. When Turbo gets to the pit, he's in last place. Luckily, the other snails know what needs to be done.

"Are you a car?" Whiplash asks him.

"No," replies Turbo.

"Then stop driving like one!" yells Whiplash. "Get out there and snail up, baby!"

Whiplash is right—a car can't do the kinds of tricks that a snail can! Turbo ducks under cars, slides up walls, and leaps past the competition and finds himself in second place.

Now it's down to Turbo and legendary racecar driver Guy Gagné.

On the last lap, Turbo bursts into the lead. Gagné is hot on his trail when the racecar driver spins out of control. He crashes into the wall. Turbo gets caught up in the crash and goes flying.

When the dust clears, Turbo looks up. He has landed right in front of the finish line!

Turbo goes to rev his engine. But nothing happens. His shell is cracked and the blue gas that gave him superspeed has seeped out!

Way up in the stands, Chet watches as Turbo curls into his shell and gives up. He can't let that happen.

"Little snail, get back here," the boy says as he watches Chet inch away.

Chet jumps out of the stands and grabs on to the string of a balloon. He floats down to the track to help his brother.

"Turbo, finish this," says Chet.

Turbo peeks out of his broken shell. "I can't," he says.

"Yes, you can," urges Chet. "It's in you. It's always been in you."

And that's all Turbo needs to hear. At a regular snail's pace, Turbo begins to inch his way toward the finish line.

Meanwhile, Gagné is pushing his crashed car toward the finish line too. Soon the two racers are neck and neck.

"Turbo!" cries Chet. "Tuck and roll!"

Turbo curls himself up into his shell and he tips over the finish line.

The spectators jump to their feet. Turbo has won the race by a shell! The little snail with big dreams is the champion of the Indy 500!

A few weeks later, everyone has returned home. Tito has a brand-new racing shell for his little amigo. When he goes to put it on, he sees that the crack in Turbo's shell has healed.

"You're all better," says Tito, placing Turbo on the starting line of the snails' new racetrack.

Chet has a new shell too, an ambulance shell. "Let's have a nice, safe race out there today, don't want any accidents," he says and then turns to Turbo. "Blow 'em off the track, bro!"

Turbo senses something he hasn't felt since the Indy 500. His shell begins to glow blue again. Could it be that his superspeed has returned? There's only one way for Turbo to find out. On your mark, get set, go!